Hansel and Gretel

This edition published 1995 by
Greenwich Editions
Unit 7, 202–208 New North Road
London N1 7BJ

Printed in Singapore

ISBN 0-8628-8017-3

Adapted by Elizabeth Hastings from Grimms' *Household Tales*
(1812-14). Text © 1992 Random House Ltd. Illustrations © 1992
Gini Wade. All rights reserved. Random House Ltd,
20 Vauxhall Bridge Road, London SW1V 2SA.

Hansel and Gretel

The Brothers Grimm

Retold by Elizabeth Hastings
Illustrated by Gini Wade

Greenwich Editions

Once upon a time a poor woodcutter lived with his family at the edge of a large forest. There was a great famine in the land and the woodcutter could not provide enough food for their needs.

One night he said to his wife, who was the children's stepmother, "What is to become of us? How are we to feed our children, Hansel and Gretel, now that we have nothing?"

"Husband," she answered, "early tomorrow morning we'll take the children into the wood. Then we shall go to our work, leaving them alone. They won't be able to find their way home, and so we shall be rid of them."

"No, wife!" said the husband. "That I won't do." But she gave him no peace till he agreed.

The children were awake, and heard what their stepmother said.

Hansel got up and stole outside. The moon was shining and the white pebbles in front of the house gleamed brightly. He filled his pockets with them.

Next morning their stepmother woke them. "Get up, you lazy ones. We are going to the forest to fetch wood."

When they had walked a little, Hansel stopped and looked back at the house. He did it again and again. Each time he dropped a little white pebble on the path.

In the middle of the forest their stepmother said, "Now lie down and rest while we go about our business."

Hansel and Gretel sat for such a long time that their eyes began to close, and soon they were fast asleep.

When they awoke it was dark, but the full moon had risen. Hansel took Gretel by the hand. They followed the pebbles, which shone in the moonlight and showed them the path. All night long they walked and in the morning they found themselves back at their father's house. When their stepmother saw them she was furious, but their father was delighted.

Soon another great famine came to the land. One night the children heard their stepmother say, "We have eaten everything. The children must go. This time we shall lead them farther into the wood so they cannot find their way out again." The father's heart was heavy, but his wife would not heed him.

When their parents were asleep, Hansel got up to go outside, but he found the door locked, and he could not get out. In the early morning the woman made the children get up. She gave them each a piece of bread. On the way to the wood, Hansel crumbled his in his pocket and every few minutes stopped and dropped a crumb to the ground, until all the bread was gone.

The woman led the children still deeper into the forest, then she said, "Just sit down here, children, and sleep for a while. We are going to cut wood."

At midday Gretel shared her bread with Hansel, who had scattered his all along the way. Then they fell asleep. It was dark when they awoke. "Wait until the moon rises. Then we shall see the breadcrumbs I scattered along the path. They will show us the way home," said Hansel.

But they could not see the crumbs, even when the moon had risen. The birds had eaten them all.

The children wandered about the whole night, and the next day also. At last they were so tired that they lay down and fell asleep.

Next morning they saw a beautiful snow-white bird on a branch.

The bird flapped its wings and flew on in front of them. They followed it until they came to a little house. With cries of joy, Hansel and Gretel saw that the house was made of gingerbread. And it had a roof of cakes, and windows made of clear sugar.

"Now," said Hansel, "we can have a feast!" He broke off a piece of the roof to see how it tasted. Gretel went to a window and began to nibble. At once a voice called out from within:

"Nibble, nibble, little mouse,
Who is nibbling at my house?"

The children answered:

"The wind, the wind,
The heaven-born wind."

And they went on eating.

Suddenly the door opened. An old, old woman, leaning on a crutch, hobbled out. Hansel and Gretel were so frightened that they dropped what they had in their hands. But the old woman only shook her head and said, "Oh, ho, you dear children! No harm shall come to you."

She took them both by the hand and led them into the house. There she gave them a delicious dinner, and after they had eaten, she showed them two little beds all ready for them.

Now, although the old woman seemed to be so friendly, she was really a wicked old witch who lay in wait for children to come by. Whenever she could get a child, she cooked him and ate him and had a real feast day.

The witch got up early in the morning. She seized Hansel, carried him into a great cage, and locked the door. Then she went back to Gretel and cried, "Get up, lazybones! Fetch some water and cook something good for your brother. When he's nice and fat, I shall eat him."

Gretel had to do what the wicked witch commanded. The best food was now cooked for poor Hansel, but Gretel had only scraps. Each morning the old woman cried, "Hansel, let me feel your finger, so that I can tell if you are getting fat."

But Hansel always held out a bone. The old woman, whose eyes were dim, wondered why he fattened so slowly.

After four weeks, the witch lost patience. "Now, then, Gretel," she called. "Hansel may be fat or thin. I'm going to cook him. First we'll do some baking. I have heated the oven and kneaded the dough." She pushed Gretel towards the oven. "Creep in and see if it is hot enough for the bread." She planned, when she had Gretel in the oven, to close the door and roast her, so that she might eat her, too.

But Gretel saw what the witch had in mind, and said, "How do I get in?"

"You silly girl," cried the witch, "the opening is big enough. See, I can get in myself." She crawled over and stuck her head into the oven. Gretel gave her a big shove and pushed her right in! Then she closed the door, and bolted it.

"Hansel!" she cried, as she opened the cage door. "We are saved! The old witch is dead." The two children danced about for joy. As they had nothing more to fear, they went into the witch's house and found chests filled with pearls and precious stones. Hansel crammed his pockets full. "I must take some too," said Gretel, and she filled her apron.

"But now we must find our way home," said Hansel.

On their way they came to a big lake. "We cannot get over this," said Hansel.

"Look, there is a white duck swimming. It will help us over, if we ask," said Gretel, and she called out,

"No boat, no bridge-alack, alack;
Please, little duck, take us on your back!"

The good duck came to them, and took them over the lake, one at a time. Then Hansel and Gretel walked on in the wood, until at long last they saw their father's house. They rushed inside and threw their arms round their father's neck. The woodcutter wept for joy, for he had not had a single happy moment since he had left them. In the meantime his wife had died.

Gretel shook out her apron and scattered pearls and precious stones all over the floor. Hansel took more jewels from his pockets. So their troubles came to an end, and they all lived together happily ever afterward.

WALT DISNEY'S
Robin Hood
and the Golden Arrow

Robin Hood and Little John were hiding out
in Sherwood Forest.

The two outlaws had tricked Prince John.
They had taken his gold and given it back
to the poor people he had robbed.

While Robin Hood stirred the kettle of soup,
Little John was hanging up the washing.

Suddenly their good friend Friar Tuck
came rushing down the road from Nottingham.

He tasted the soup.

Then he said, "Have you heard the news?
Prince John is holding an archery contest.
All the archers in the kingdom are invited.
And Maid Marian will give the golden arrow
to the one who wins the contest."

Robin Hood was very happy to hear the news.

"I will go to that contest," he shouted.
"And I will win the golden arrow and see Maid
Marian too!"

"Wait a minute, Robin," said Friar Tuck. "How
can you go to Prince John's contest? All of his
soldiers will be waiting for you!"

"Don't worry," Robin answered.
"No one will know who we are.
We will wear disguises."

Robin dressed up like a long-legged stork.

Little John dressed himself to look like
a nobleman of high rank.

Who would believe they were
really two famous outlaws?

On their way to the archery contest, they met the Sheriff of Nottingham.

"Why, good morning, Sheriff," said Robin. "What an honor to meet you here."

"And a good morning to you, my fine friend," answered the sheriff.

He never guessed that he was speaking to Robin Hood!

As Robin and Little John drew near the castle grounds, they met all sorts of people.

Everyone in the kingdom was coming to Prince John's archery contest.

In the center of the field stood a very tall
throne.

Prince John was sitting there beside Sir Hiss,
his advisor.

Prince John smiled.

"At last we are going to capture that outlaw Robin Hood," he said.

"Are you quite sure, sire?" asked Sir Hiss.

"Of course I am sure. Robin Hood loves Maid Marian. So I know he will come and try to win the golden arrow."

"You should be careful," warned Sir Hiss.

"Remember how Robin Hood and Little John stole the rings right off your fingers ... and the wheels right off your coach."

"Silence, Hiss!" roared the prince. "And don't ever let your head be higher than mine!"

The line of archers marched across the field.
They had come from all over the kingdom.
Each archer carried a stout-looking bow.

At the end of the line walked a tall archer
on stilt-like legs.

He was right in front of the sheriff.

Little John did not stay with Robin Hood.

He went straight to Prince John and bowed low
before him.

"And who might you be, sire?" asked Sir Hiss.

"I am Sir Reginald, Duke of Chutney," answered
Little John. "I have come to pay my respects
to Prince John."

"Please sit down, sir," said the prince.
"We do not often get such fine visitors."

Little John sat down
—right on Sir Hiss.

"Sir Chutney! You
have taken MY seat,"
said Hiss.

"Hiss! Get out
of here!" commanded
Prince John. "You are
no longer needed.

Go out onto the field and keep
your eyes open for that villain
Robin Hood."

Just then Maid Marian came
up to the throne with Lady Kluck.
They bowed to Prince John.
Then they sat down next
to the royal throne and waited
for the archers to file past.

One archer, taller than the others, handed
a flower to Maid Marian.

"It is a great honor," he said, "to be
shooting for a lovely lady like you."

Then he winked at her and walked away.

"My goodness, Kluck," said Maid Marian.
"The eyes of that archer
do look familiar."

Suddenly the trumpeters on the castle tower
blew their horns.

The archery contest was about to begin.

The contest master walked toward the throne.
He stopped in front of Prince John and held
up the golden arrow on its purple cushion.

The archers lined up in a long, straight row, ready to shoot.

At the signal each one, in turn, let his arrow
fly toward the target.

The sheriff and the stork were the best.

The sheriff's arrow went right into the center
of the yellow circle.

But Robin Hood's arrow went right into the
circle too.

The first match had ended in a tie.

Little John looked at the prince.

"Did you see that?" he asked. "That long-legged archer is very good!"

"Indeed he is." The prince smiled. "I just wonder who he can be. Not many men can shoot as well as the sheriff."

On the field the sheriff and Robin Hood
were getting ready for their next shot.

"I hear you are having trouble catching
that rascal Robin Hood," said the long-legged
archer.

"Oh, it's no trouble," said the sheriff.
"He's scared of me, that's all. But if he
dares to come here today, I will spot him—
even in one of those silly disguises."

"Attention, everyone!"
shouted the contest master.
"The sheriff and the stork
from Devonshire will shoot
again. But first they must
move back thirty paces."

The sheriff bowed
very low.

Then the stork bowed,
at the same time waving
to Maid Marian.

Maid Marian waved back.
She was smiling happily.
Now she was sure that she
knew who the long-legged
archer was.

"I think you like that tall archer,"
said Prince John.

"Oh, yes!" answered Maid Marian, and
her face turned red. "That is, he makes
me smile."

But the prince was not smiling. For
now he was sure that he knew who the
long-legged archer was.

It was the sheriff's turn to shoot again.
This time his arrow went too high.
But the target holder quickly raised
the target.

The arrow landed in the bull's-eye!

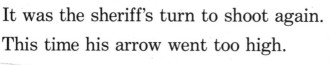

Next, the stork took his turn.
The long-legged archer aimed carefully and
stretched his bowstring tight.
His arrow flew straight to the bull's-eye.

It knocked the sheriff's
arrow to the ground.

The stork had won!

Friar Tuck roared with delight.
"He did it! He did it!"
All the villagers cheered with him.
The long-legged stork from Devonshire
was the hero of the day.

Maid Marian hugged
Lady Kluck.

Prince John
whispered an order
to the contest master.

The contest master
whispered the order
to the captain
of the rhino
guards.

Robin Hood walked to the throne and
bowed to Prince John.

"Archer," said the prince, "you have won
the contest. Now you will get your reward!"

With a quick slash of his sword,
the prince tore off Robin's stork
disguise.

All the rhino guards grabbed Robin and
tied him round and round with ropes.

"Robin Hood, I have been waiting to catch
you," shouted Prince John. "Now that I have
you, you shall die!"

"Oh, no, Prince John," cried Maid Marian. "Spare his life, I beg of you."

"Why should I?" asked the prince.

"Because I love him," Maid Marian answered softly.

While Maid Marian was talking, Little John quietly sneaked behind the throne.

All at once Prince John felt something
sharp sticking into his back. And a strong
hand pulled his collar tight around his
neck.

"All right, Prince," whispered Little John.
"Tell your men to let Robin Hood go."

"Untie the prisoner!"
shouted the prince. "Let
him go at once, I say!"

Suddenly Robin Hood was free again.

The sheriff could not believe what
was happening.

Before Prince John could change his mind,
Robin rushed to the platform and grabbed Maid
Marian and Lady Kluck.

Running behind the throne, Robin Hood took
the dagger from Little John.

Then he cut the rope that held the cloth
roof over the throne.

Down it crashed, trapping the prince,
the sheriff, and all of the guards.

While the prince and his men struggled to get free, Robin and his three friends ran off as fast as they could go.

They did not stop running until they were
across the river, safe in the shelter of the
forest.

"You see," said Robin. "I did win the contest."

And that was how Maid Marian and Lady Kluck
came to join Robin Hood and his band of outlaws
in Sherwood Forest.